DRAGONSITTER
TROUBLE

The Dragonsitter's Island first published by
Andersen Press in 2014
The Dragonsitter's Party first published by
Andersen Press in 2015

This bind-up edition first published in 2015 by
Andersen Press Limited
20 Vauxhall Bridge Road
London SW1V 2SA
www.andersenpress.co.uk

2 4 6 8 10 9 7 5 3 1

British Library Cataloguing in Publication Data available.

ISBN 978 1 78344 297 3

Printed and bound in Great Britain by CPI Group (UK) Ltd,
Croydon CR0 4YY

DRAGONSITTER TROUBLE

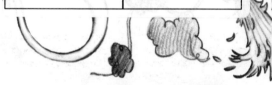

Josh Lacey

Illustrated by Garry Parsons

Andersen Press
London

Contents

The
Dragonsitter's
Island

From: Edward Smith–Pickle
To: Morton Pickle
Date: Saturday 18 February
Subject: Please read this!

Attachments: Your new front door

Dear Uncle Morton

Where is the key to your house?

We arrived on your island this morning, but we couldn't get in.

Mum thought you might have left it under a stone or buried in a flowerpot, so we searched everywhere.

Emily discovered a silver necklace and I found one pound, but there was no sign of the key.

Through the window I could see your dragons going crazy. I don't know if they were happy to see us or just hungry, but Arthur was charging round and round the house, knocking over your furniture, and Ziggy wouldn't stop breathing fire.

3

Luckily Mr McDougall was still here. He was sure you wouldn't mind if he broke a window.

Unfortunately he couldn't open the front door from the inside, so we had to push the suitcases through the window and climb in after them.

Ziggy and Arthur are much happier now we've given them our presents (a big box of Maltesers for her and three packets of chocolate mini eggs for him).

They also ate our leftover sandwiches from the train and the book I was reading. Luckily it wasn't very good.

Emily and I are going to search your house for the key. Mum says if we can't find it, we'll have to go home tomorrow and the dragons can fend for themselves.

I said I wouldn't mind climbing in and out of the window for the whole week, but Mum told me not to be ridiculous.

Have you taken it by mistake? Didn't you leave a spare anywhere?

Love from

Your favourite nephew

Eddie

Dear Uncle Morton

We haven't found the key, but I have found your phone. Mum rang you to leave another message and I heard it ringing behind the sofa.

I hope you don't need it in Outer Mongolia. I put it on the mantelpiece with the necklace and the pound.

Mr McDougall has gone back to the mainland in his boat. Emily says it's creepy being the only people here, but I like it.

Thanks for your instructions and the map. Emily and Mum took hours unpacking their bags, so I've been exploring.
I climbed Dead Man's Cairn and walked all the way along the beach to Lookout Point.

Arthur sat on my shoulder like a parrot. At first I was worried he might burn my ear off, but he hasn't been breathing any fire at all. Isn't he old enough?

Eddie

From: Edward Smith-Pickle

To: Morton Pickle

Date: Saturday 18 February

Subject: Tins

📎 **Attachments:** Accidental number 2

Dear Uncle Morton

We have now searched your house, your garden and quite a lot of your island, but we still can't find the key. Please write back ASAP and tell us where it is.

Mum is deadly serious about leaving tomorrow. It's not just because of the key. It's the poos too. Ziggy did one in the kitchen and another by the back door.

I know it's not her fault. She can't fit through the window and she has to go somewhere. I just wish she could hold them in till we've found the key.

Also Mum says where is the tin opener?

We brought some food, but not enough because you told us your cupboard was full of provisions. Unfortunately all the provisions are in tins.

I'm sure I could open them with a knife but Mum won't let me because we'd need a helicopter to get to the nearest hospital.

Eddie

From: Edward Smith-Pickle

To: Morton Pickle

Date: Sunday 19 February

Subject: Bye

Attachments: The red flag

Dear Uncle Morton

I'm very sorry, but we are leaving your island.

This morning Mum found another poo in the kitchen. She said that was the final straw.

I did suggest staying here on my own, but Mum said, "Not a chance, buster."

She has already raised the red flag. I just looked through the telescope and saw Mr McDougall preparing his boat on the mainland. I suppose he'll be here in about fifteen minutes.

I have given all our spare food to the dragons. I have also put some tins on the floor in case they're better at opening them than me.

I will ask Mr McDougall to come here every day and feed them till you get back.

Eddie

From: Edward Smith–Pickle

To: Morton Pickle

Date: Sunday 19 February

Subject: Sheep

Attachments: The prime suspects

Dear Uncle Morton

We're still here.

We never left. Mr McDougall wouldn't let us.

He said the dragons can't stay on your island unsupervised.

Mum asked why not, and Mr McDougall explained that one of his sheep went missing in the middle of the night. This morning he found bloodstains on the grass and a trail of wool leading down to the water.

I don't know why he blames your dragons. Arthur can hardly fly and Ziggy can't even leave the house, so there is no way either

12

of them could have got from here to the
mainland, let alone murdered a sheep.
But Mr McDougall says they are the prime
suspects.

Now he has gone home again and we're
stuck here without a key or any food.

Eddie

From: Morton Pickle

To: Edward Smith–Pickle

Date: Monday 20 February

Subject: Re: Sheep

📎 **Attachments:** The library; Airag and stew

Dear Eddie

I am so sorry to hear about your troubles with the front door. I was sure that I had discussed the key with your mother when we talked last week. Has she forgotten our conversation?

This is what I said to her. If you walk down to the end of the garden, you will discover a stone statue of a Yellow-headed Vulture perched in the heather. The key is hidden under its left talon.

Please be very careful when you lift it up. That vulture has great sentimental value. I was given it by the sculptor himself, who lives in a small hut beside the Amazon, and I carried it all the way back from Brazil wrapped in an old shirt.

14

I have been in touch with Mr McDougall, who is understandably upset about the loss of his sheep. I assured him that the dragons couldn't be responsible. He didn't appear to be entirely convinced, but I'm sure he'll find the real culprit soon.

All is good here in Ulaanbaatar. I have discovered some fascinating and unexpected information in the National Library, so my visit has already been worthwhile.

The only problem is the weather. Walking the streets without a coat would be certain death and even the Reading Room is so cold that no one removes their hats or scarves.

Unfortunately it's impossible to turn the pages of an old book while wearing gloves, so my fingers are like icicles by the end of the day. Every evening, after leaving the library, I warm myself up in a local restaurant with a bowl of yak stew and a glass of the local brew – a white drink called airag, made from fermented horse milk. It tastes better than it sounds.

I'm very sorry about the tin opener. Have you looked in the cutlery drawer?

With love from

Your affectionate uncle

Morton

From: Edward Smith-Pickle

To: Morton Pickle

Date: Monday 20 February

Subject: Speedboat

Attachments: Mum and Emily

Dear Uncle Morton

We found the key!

And we were very careful with the statue.

Mum says you definitely didn't mention it last week. She would have remembered if you had.

You don't have to worry about the tin opener. It wasn't in the cutlery drawer or anywhere else, but Mr McDougall's nephew Gordon nipped across this morning in his speedboat and delivered another. He also brought a box of oatcakes and some nice cheese.

After he had gone, I found Mum and Emily whispering in the kitchen.

17

When I asked what was going on, Emily
said they were talking about Gordon. Mum
thinks he's very handsome.

I don't know if he's handsome, but I like his
boat. He said he'll take me for a ride round
the island to see the puffins.

Love from

Eddie

From: Edward Smith-Pickle
To: Morton Pickle
Date: Tuesday 21 February
Subject: More sheep

Dear Uncle Morton

Gordon has been here again. He took us to Lower Bisket in his speedboat to buy provisions.

Emily thinks it was a date.

Mum told her not to be ridiculous, but she did go bright pink.

Apparently Mr McDougall is on the rampage. Another sheep went missing last night.

I asked Gordon to tell him that the dragons spent the whole night in my bedroom with the door shut and the windows locked.

Gordon said I should do the same tonight because Mr McDougall is planning to stay up from dusk till dawn with a Thermos of hot tea and a rifle.

Otherwise everything is fine. We bought lots of food in the Lower Bisket General Store. The dragons are happy. Even Mum is in a good mood. We went for a walk on the beach this afternoon and she said it's so peaceful and beautiful she can almost understand why you want to live here.

Eddie

From: Morton Pickle
To: Edward Smith-Pickle
Date: Tuesday 21 February
Subject: Re: More sheep

Dear Eddie

I have to admit that I was worried by your last message. I know from personal experience that Mr McDougall is an excellent shot.

On that particular occasion he wasn't aiming at me, but I should not like to find myself in his sights.

Please make sure that you keep the dragons under observation at all times. I cannot believe that they could be responsible for attacking his livestock but I wouldn't want to expose them to any unnecessary risks.

I hope your mother enjoyed her date with Gordon. Isn't he a little young for her?

Morton

From: Edward Smith-Pickle

To: Morton Pickle

Date: Wednesday 22 February

Subject: Fish

Attachments: The Fish Museum

Dear Uncle Morton

You don't have to worry about the dragons. I am keeping a close eye on them.

This morning I took them for a walk along the beach and I didn't let them out of my sight for a moment.

I told Mum what you said about Gordon being too young for her, and she said actually the age difference is only two years and ten months.

Today he took us to the Fish Museum in Arbothnot. He said it's the biggest attraction in the area.

I suppose it would be very interesting if you liked fish.

Afterwards Gordon bought us souvenirs in the museum shop. He got a plastic shark for me and a marine sticker book for Emily. He wanted to buy a pair of pearl earrings for Mum but she said they were too expensive, so he got her some smoked salmon instead.

He is coming back tomorrow for tea.

Emily asked if we would have to move to Scotland if they got married. Mum just laughed and said we will cross that bridge when we come to it.

Love from

Eddie

Dear Uncle Morton

The McDougalls are here.

Mum actually only invited Gordon but Mr McDougall came too.

He won't stop shouting and waving his arms.

He has lost three sheep in a week. Now he wants to take the dragons away and lock them in his barn till the police arrive.

I said he couldn't do that, but he said, "Don't you worry, laddie, it's perfectly legal."

I can't understand how it can be perfectly legal to steal someone else's dragons, but no one is taking any notice of me.

If you get this, please call us ASAP.

Someone has to stop Mr McDougall!

Eddie

From: Edward Smith–Pickle

To: Morton Pickle

Date: Thursday 23 February

Subject: Your shed

Attachments: The prisoners

Dear Uncle Morton

The McDougalls have gone.

Everyone argued for a long time and finally Mr McDougall agreed the dragons could stay here as long as they're locked up.

They are now in the shed.

Arthur is miserable. He keeps screaming and wailing and bashing his head against the door, trying to break it open.

I told him he's only in there for his own safety but he took no notice.

Mum says he'll calm down when he's had something to eat. We're going to open a few tins and give the dragons a special supper.

I hope Mr McDougall catches the sheep thief soon.

Eddie

From: Edward Smith-Pickle

To: Morton Pickle

Date: Friday 24 February

Subject: Missing

📎 **Attachments:** The only fireman on the island

Dear Uncle Morton

I'm very sorry, but your dragons have burned down your shed.

Emily and I were having breakfast when we smelled smoke. We ran outside and saw the whole thing blazing.

I put out the fire with buckets of water but there's not much left except a few black bits of wood.

There's no sign of your dragons either.

I'm afraid I can't build your shed again. I'm terrible at woodwork. Last time we did it at school, I put a nail through my knee.

But I will find your dragons, I promise.

Eddie

From: Edward Smith–Pickle

To: Morton Pickle

Date: Friday 24 February

Subject: Look!

Attachments: The real sheep thief

Dear Uncle Morton

I have discovered who has been eating Mr McDougall's sheep!

It is the Loch Ness Monster.

I was actually looking for your dragons. I finally found them on the beach, mucking about on the sand as if nothing had happened. They didn't even look guilty.

I was just about to give them a proper telling-off when I happened to look out to sea, and I saw this!

I shall tell Mr McDougall as soon as I see him.

Eddie

From: Morton Pickle

To: Edward Smith-Pickle

Date: Friday 24 February

Subject: Re: Look!

Dear Eddie

Thank you for the photo. I'm not an expert, but I would say it's a swan.

Don't worry about Mr McDougall's sheep or who might be eating them. Keeping the dragons safe is much more important. Could you lock them in the house?

Of course you'll have to let them out every now and then to stretch their wings and go to the loo, but please make sure they don't run away again.

The livestock laws are very clear. If Mr McDougall caught them anywhere near his sheep, he would have a perfect right to shoot them.

My work here is almost done. Last night

I was lucky enough to have dinner with Professor Ganbaataryn Baast, and he has invited me to accompany him on an expedition to the Altai mountains this summer, searching for a famous family of dragons. Apparently they live in an enormous cave stuffed with gold. No man has ever seen it and lived to tell the tale. Professor Baast intends to be the first – and I shall be the second!

Morton

From: Edward Smith-Pickle

To: Morton Pickle

Date: Friday 24 February

Subject: Famous Mysteries

Dear Uncle Morton

It is not a swan. It's definitely the Loch Ness Monster. I've got a book about Famous Mysteries at home and I recognise it from the pictures.

I'm going to search your island for it.

If I get a better photo, I can prove to Mr McDougall who has really been stealing his sheep, and he'll stop blaming Ziggy and Arthur.

I asked Mum and Emily to help but they're not interested. They don't even believe I've seen the Loch Ness Monster.

In fact Mum thinks I'm making up stories because of Gordon.

After lunch she sat me down for a serious talk. She said Gordon isn't her boyfriend but she might get a boyfriend one day and would I mind?

I said Dad has a new girlfriend every time we see him, so who cares?

Anyway, even if I was upset about Mum having a boyfriend, why would I make up stories about the Loch Ness Monster?

Eddie

Dear Uncle Morton

I borrowed your boat. I hope you don't mind. I was very careful.

I took the dragons too. I know you want them to stay locked up, but they'll actually be safer with me. I won't let them out of my sight.

We rowed into the middle of the sea, but there was no sign of the monster.

I would have rowed the whole way round the island, but I didn't want to get swept out to sea. So I rowed back to your jetty and tied up the boat, then started walking.

I found:

A bird's nest with three eggs.

A whole tree washed up on the beach.

A wrecked boat buried in the sand.

A starfish (dead).

Six crabs (still alive).

Some puffins.

And about a thousand seagulls.

Unfortunately there was no sign of Nessie.

Do you know any caves where she might be hiding?

Eddie

From: Morton Pickle
To: Edward Smith–Pickle
Date: Friday 24 February
Subject: Re: Nessie

Dear Eddie

Please don't be offended if I say this, but I really don't think you have seen the Loch Ness Monster.

A few years ago, I made a study of the myths and legends surrounding that fabulous beast. I wondered whether it might be a dragon, or a distant relative of the dragon which had somehow become aquatic.

Sadly I discovered that there is no reliable evidence that the monster has ever existed. All the sightings are, I'm afraid to say, the work of drunks, maniacs, frauds, fantasists and publicity-seekers of one sort or another.

I wish the monster did exist, but it doesn't. And even if it did, it would be swimming around Loch Ness, not my island.

In the years that I've been living there, I have spotted whales, dolphins, seals and even the occasional otter, so you may have been lucky enough to see one of them.

I don't know who or what has been stealing Mr McDougall's sheep but I can tell you one thing for certain: it is not Nessie.

Morton

If the monster doesn't exist, what's this?

Eddie

From: Morton Pickle

To: Edward Smith-Pickle

Date: Friday 24 February

Subject: Re: Re: Re: Nessie

I'm coming home! Will change my tickets and catch next plane!

Do not approach the monster till I get there! It might be dangerous!

M

From: Edward Smith-Pickle

To: Morton Pickle

Date: Saturday 25 February

Subject: On the beach

Attachments: Flying practice; Air raid

Dear Uncle Morton

You're right about the monster. It is dangerous. In fact it's bloodthirsty.

It just tried to eat Arthur.

Ziggy was curled up on the sofa with Emily and Mum, watching some old movie. Arthur and I didn't want to see it so we went down on the beach again. I was using your binoculars to search for the Loch Ness Monster and Arthur was practising his flying.

He kept running along the sand and jumping into the air, then flapping his wings to stay up for as long as possible.

I tried to persuade him to land on the beach because rescuing him from the water is no fun at all, but he didn't take much notice.

One time he veered in the wrong direction and headed straight out to sea. I called at him to come back but he just flew further and further from the shore, as if he was trying to get all the way to the mainland.

Suddenly there was a great burst of water and the monster rose out of the waves, its long neck stretching into the air and its huge mouth opening to reveal two rows of glistening white teeth.

Snap!

It tried to take a bite out of Arthur. Just in time he dodged out of the way.

Snap! Snap!

The monster went for him again and again. Each time Arthur twisted through the air like a fighter pilot. I'd never seen him move so fast.

Finally he managed to point himself in the right direction and head back to the shore.

The monster charged after him. Both of them were coming straight for me.

Once they reached dry land, the monster couldn't move so quickly. It just waddled up the shore, flapping its flippers on the sand.

Arthur crashlanded at my feet. I could see he was absolutely exhausted by the effort of so much flying. I picked him up and tucked him under my arm and we ran all the way home.

From now on I'm going to follow your advice. I won't go anywhere near the monster till you get back.

Eddie

Dear Eddie

I am writing this from Ulaanbaatar airport. The runways are covered in thick snow and slippery ice, so my flight has been delayed. Apparently we should be boarding within the next hour.

I have to change planes in Moscow and Copenhagen, but if all goes well I shall be back in Edinburgh tomorrow morning and home in time for lunch.

I'm glad to hear you're going to keep away from the monster. Perhaps you should stay inside the house till I get back.

Morton

Dear Uncle Morton

You don't have to come home early if you don't want to.

Everything is fine here now. The monster has gone and Mr McDougall has forgiven your dragons.

He wasn't so friendly earlier. He arrived in his rowing boat with Gordon, ready to arrest Ziggy and Arthur.

He had been watching us through his binoculars and saw them snoozing on the grass. He said if we couldn't keep them safely locked up, he would take them straight to the police station in Upper Bucket.

I told him it was actually the Loch Ness Monster who had been stealing his sheep.

He just laughed and said, "Are you sure, laddie? You don't think it's those aliens from outer space?"

I said he should come and see the monster for himself, and he said maybe he would after he'd arrested the dragons.

He tied a rope round Arthur's neck and marched him down to the boat. Ziggy kept snapping at his legs and blowing little spurts of flame in his direction, but she didn't bite his head off or set him on fire. I suppose she was worried about hurting Arthur too.

Gordon tried to stop his uncle, and so did Mum, but Mr McDougall wouldn't listen. He said he couldn't afford to lose another sheep and did they want to bankrupt him?

When we got to the jetty, Mr McDougall put Arthur in the bottom of the boat and

Ziggy jumped in after them. I tried to climb in too, but Gordon grabbed me round the middle and said, "Not so fast."

Mr McDougall dipped his oars and rowed out to sea. We were all shouting at him – me and Emily and Mum and Gordon – but he took no notice. He just headed for the mainland.

The waves got bigger. The boat was rolling around. I was really worried it might tip over and Arthur would drown.

They were almost halfway between the island and the mainland when the monster attacked. It seemed to come from nowhere. It lifted its head out of the water, opened its mouth and lunged at them.

Mr McDougall tried to defend himself with one of the oars but the monster bit the end off. Then it took a big chunk out of the boat.

It would have eaten them all if Ziggy hadn't fought back. She was amazing!

She flapped her wings and lifted into the air, then breathed a great big ball of fire straight at the monster's head.

I've never seen anyone look so surprised.

The monster floated there for a moment, its scales smouldering. Then it raised itself out of the waves and struck again.

The battle was terrible. But I always knew who would win. And I was right.

Every time the monster tried to bite Ziggy, she flew out of its way, then turned round and blew back another blazing fireball. Soon the Loch Ness Monster was black and burnt and smoking from the top of its head to the tip of its tail.

Finally it plunged under the waves and disappeared in a cloud of bubbles.

Ziggy dragged Arthur and Mr McDougall back to shore. She couldn't swim very fast with them holding her wings but that didn't matter. At least they were safe.

Mr McDougall wasn't very happy about leaving his boat behind, but it was already smashed to pieces and just about to sink.

When they finally got to the beach, Mr McDougall lay on the sand for a minute or two, getting his breath back. Then he rolled over and said, "I owe you an apology, laddie."

I told him my name is actually Eddie and he promised to call me that from now on.

He said sorry to the dragons too.

Now we're all inside your house. I hope you don't mind, but Mr McDougall has borrowed some of your dry clothes.

Mum is making cocoa for everyone, the dragons included.

Eddie

Hi E

I'm changing planes in Moscow.

Just checked timetables and should be home on 15.37 train – could you ask Gordon to meet me?

Glad to hear you're all safe. Please be very careful till I get there. The monster might come back.

M

Dear Uncle Morton

You don't have to worry about the monster. I'm sure it won't be coming back.

Even if it does, Ziggy will chase it away again.

Gordon came to meet your train at 15.37 but there was no sign of you. Did you miss your plane?

We have been packing up and getting ready to leave tomorrow.

I'd like to stay on your island for another week but school starts on Tuesday, so Mum says we have to go home.

Eddie

From: Edward Smith-Pickle

To: Morton Pickle

Date: Sunday 26 February

Subject: Our last night

Attachments: The jetty; The beach

Dear Uncle Morton

Gordon got your message about the plane and the train. He will be waiting for you tomorrow at 9.01.

Our train leaves at 9.27, so we'll just have time to say hello and goodbye.

We're all packed and ready to go. I'm very sad to be leaving your island but our last night has been brilliant. We had a barbecue on the beach – Mr McDougall, the dragons, Emily and me.

Mum wasn't there. She went to a restaurant on the mainland with Gordon.

This time it really was a date. Mum was very worried because she hadn't brought

any smart clothes, but Emily and I told her it didn't matter because she looked beautiful how she was.

And she did. When she was standing on the jetty, waiting for Gordon to pick her up in his speedboat, she looked like someone in a movie.

Once they'd gone, Emily and I collected driftwood on the beach, Ziggy lit the fire and Mr McDougall cooked the best barbie ever.

Mr McDougall has entirely forgiven your dragons. He says Ziggy is a bonnie lass and she's welcome to as many lamb cutlets as she wants.

The McDougalls have gone home now but they're coming back to pick us up in the morning.

See you tomorrow!

Eddie

From: Morton Pickle

To: Edward Smith–Pickle

Date: Tuesday 28 February

Subject: Re: Our last night

Attachments: Two happy dragons

Dear Eddie

I was so sorry to miss you yesterday. My plane was delayed again and I finally got to the station at three o'clock in the afternoon. Luckily Gordon was still waiting for me.

Ziggy and Arthur are both in fine spirits.

They've obviously had a very happy week.
Thank you for looking after them so well.

I brought some presents from Outer
Mongolia to say thank you. I shall send
them by first class post.

The McDougalls and I patrolled the
shore last night, armed with torches and
shotguns, but the monster did not return.
I do hope she'll come back soon. I would
love to see her for myself.

As you know, Gordon was eager to contact
the newspapers but I persuaded him not
to. For one thing, I don't want hordes of
reporters swarming across my island.
For another, despite her ferocity, Nessie
deserves some privacy.

Apparently Mr McDougall did tell the whole
pub about her but everyone just thought
he'd had too many whiskies.

We have now agreed she will remain our
secret. I suggest you do the same.

I have not quizzed Gordon on other matters but I gather he has been in touch with your mother, and may be visiting you at some point. Perhaps he could bring the dragons? Or would you like to come and stay again? All of us would be delighted to see you.

Morton

From: Edward Smith-Pickle

To: Morton Pickle

Date: Thursday 2 March

Subject: Home

Attachments: Scarf; Slippers

Dear Uncle Morton

We're back home too. Our house and our garden feel very small compared to your island, but it's nice to see my stuff again.

I think you're right about keeping quiet about the monster. My book about Famous Mysteries says Loch Ness is packed with scientists and tourists. You wouldn't want them on your island. In fact, that's probably why she decided to leave Loch Ness in the first place.

I had already shown the photos to Miss Brackenbury, but I've asked her not to tell anyone. She said our secret is safe with her.

Thank you very much for the presents from
Outer Mongolia. Emily has been wearing
her cashmere scarf non-stop, and I really
like my slipper. Please do send the other
one if you discover where Arthur hid it.

Mum hasn't tried the airag yet. She's keeping it for a special occasion.

I talked to Mum about coming back to your island and she says we'll see. That usually means no, but I think this time it might mean yes.

Love from

Eddie

Hi Eddie

I was sent this by a friend in Australia and thought you might be interested!

M

ADELAIDE DAILY NEWS

Tuesday 23rd May

Dinosaur spotted on popular Adelaide beach

Swimmers and holidaymakers were shocked yesterday by the sudden appearance of a mysterious beast on Semaphore Beach.

More than a hundred people fled from the water when an unidentified creature was spotted swimming about twenty metres from the shore.

Reports say that the beast had a small head, a long neck, an enormous brown body and little flippers. Some witnesses described it as looking like a dinosaur, leading experts to wonder if a previously unknown species could have been living on the shores of Australia for the past sixty million years.

Beachgoers have been warned to stay out of the water all along Adelaide's beachfront until scientists and experts have studied photographs and footage of the unknown intruder. No one was hurt and the creature only stayed for a few minutes, leading to speculation that it might have been a trick of the light, a strangely-shaped piece of driftwood or even a great white shark covered in seaweed.

Local resident Gav McPherson remains baffled. "We're used to sharks and sea lions here. Killer jellyfish are no problem either. But this was something else, mate. I've never seen anything like it."

Police Chief Tina O'Sullivan says her department is keeping an open mind until further investigations have been completed. She refused to comment on speculation that the sighting could be linked to a series of sheep thefts in the area.

The Dragonsitter's Party

ABRACADABRA!
KAZAM KAZOOM!!
PREPARE TO BE AMAZED!!!

The world-famous master of magic

★ Mister Mysterio ★

will be appearing at Eddie's birthday party

COME AND SEE HIS
INCREDIBLE TRICKS
YOU WILL NOT BELIEVE YOUR EYES!

At: Eddie's house

On: Saturday 25th March   From: 3pm to 5pm

Please RSVP to: Eddie's mum

Dear Uncle Morton

Did you get my invitation?

I just wanted to check because you're the only person who hasn't RSVPed.

I hope you can come. It's going to be a great party. We're having a magician.

Love from

your favourite nephew

Eddie

From: Morton Pickle

To: Edward Smith–Pickle

Date: Tuesday 21 March

Subject: Re: My party

Dear Eddie

I would have loved to have come to your party. There is very little that I enjoy more than the work of a good magician.

Unfortunately I have already promised to stay in Scotland and help on the farm with Mr McDougall, who is a man short this weekend.

That man is, of course, our mutual friend Gordon, who is very excited about coming to see you. He talks about nothing else.

I can hardly believe that he only met your mother a few weeks ago. He already seems to know much more about her than I do, and I've known her for an entire lifetime.

Mr McDougall only agreed to give Gordon the weekend off if I would work in his place. It is the lambing season here and the farm has never been busier.

He will be bringing a small birthday surprise for you.

With love from

your affectionate uncle

Morton

From: Edward Smith-Pickle

To: Morton Pickle

Date: Wednesday 22 March

Subject: Your surprise

 Attachments: Emily

Dear Uncle Morton

Thank you for the surprise. I can't wait to see what it is.

Mum is very excited about Gordon coming to visit. She keeps buying new dresses, then taking them back to the shop because they're not quite right.

I'm sorry you can't come to my party. I know my friends would like to meet you. Will you come next year instead?

I'll send you some pictures of Mister Mysterio sawing someone in half.

Apparently that's the best bit of his act.

I am going to suggest he does Emily.

She said, "That's not funny," and I said I wasn't trying to be funny. I just thought the house would be a bit more peaceful if I only had half a sister.

Love from

Eddie

From: Edward Smith-Pickle

To: Morton Pickle

Date: Thursday 23 March

Subject: Special time

Attachments: They're here!

Dear Uncle Morton

Gordon has arrived with your surprise.

Mum was definitely surprised, but not in a good way.

She said if she'd wanted your dragons to come and stay, she would have invited them.

She was hoping to spend some special time with Gordon this weekend, but she says their time isn't going to be very special if she's got to look after two dragons, not to mention the nineteen kids who will be descending on the house on Saturday afternoon.

Of course I was very happy to see them.

I can't believe how much Arthur has grown!

He's also getting quite good at flying. We put him in the garden in case he needed a poo after the long drive and he almost got over the wall.

It's lucky he didn't, because Mrs Kapelski was pruning her roses, and she has a weak heart.

I do wish Ziggy and Arthur could stay for my party. I know my friends would like to meet them.

But Mum said, "Not a chance, buster."

Could you come and get them ASAP?

Love from

Eddie

From: Edward Smith–Pickle

To: Morton Pickle

Date: Thursday 23 March

Subject: Dinner

Attachments: I don't do pets

Dear Uncle Morton

I just rang both your numbers, but there was no answer. Are you already on your way to collect the dragons?

I hope so, because Mum says they are living on borrowed time.

She and Gordon were meant to be going out for dinner in a posh French restaurant. Mum was wearing her best new dress and Gordon looked very nice in his suit.

But the babysitter took one look at Arthur and said, "I don't do pets."

We promised to lock Arthur upstairs in my bedroom with Ziggy, but she wouldn't change her mind, even when Mum offered to pay her double.

85

By that time it was too late to get another
babysitter, so Mum had to cancel the
reservation.

Luckily she had two steaks in the fridge, so they decided to stay here and have a nice romantic evening in front of the telly.

Unluckily she took the steaks out of the fridge, put them on the side and turned round to get the vegetables.

By the time she turned back again, Ziggy had eaten one steak and Arthur was half-way through the other.

So she's ordered a curry.

Gordon says he likes curry much more than French food, but I think he's just trying to be nice.

Please call us ASAP and tell us your ETA.

Eddie

PS If you don't know what ETA means, it means Estimated Time of Arrival.

From: Edward Smith-Pickle

To: Morton Pickle

Date: Thursday 23 March

Subject: Curry

Attachments: Mum in a mood

Dear Uncle Morton

Arthur ate the curry.

I didn't actually see it happen because I was upstairs cleaning my teeth, but I heard the screams.

Mum says if you're not here first thing tomorrow morning, she's going to put your dragons on the train and send them back to Scotland on their own.

To be honest, I can understand why she's so upset.

She's been looking forward to her date with Gordon for ages and your dragons have just ruined it.

She won't even let them into the house.

88

She chased them onto the patio with a broom and says they have to stay there all night.

I wanted to stay with them in my sleeping bag, but Mum says I'll catch my death of cold.

I hope the dragons don't catch theirs.

Eddie

From: Morton Pickle

To: Edward Smith-Pickle

Date: Thursday 23 March

Subject: Re: Curry

Dear Eddie

I'm terribly sorry I haven't replied to your recent messages, but it's all hands on deck for the lambing here.

Please tell your mother that I am very sorry. I had thought the dragons would be a nice birthday surprise for you. I didn't realise that they would spoil her weekend with Gordon.

Of course I shall come and collect them. I have just checked the timetables. If I leave my island at dawn and row to the mainland, I can get to the station in time for the first train and should be with you by the evening.

However, I have already promised my services to Mr McDougall for the entire weekend, so I can only leave him in the lurch if Gordon comes straight back here and does the lambing himself.

Unless your mother would prefer him to stay where he is?

Morton

PS Your mother is quite right: however warm your sleeping bag may be, you will be much more comfortable in your own bed. There is no need to be concerned about Ziggy and Arthur. They are used to Scottish winters and Outer Mongolian blizzards, so a short spell in the garden won't do them any harm.

Dear Uncle Morton

I told Mum what you said. She thought about it for a bit. Then she said, "Fine."

I think she must really like Gordon.

Mum even let the dragons back inside.

I just hope the smell doesn't make her change her mind.

Arthur has been doing terrible farts all morning. The whole house stinks of curry.

He'd better stop before tomorrow or my friends will be poisoned.

Now they're having porridge for breakfast.

I wouldn't have thought dragons liked porridge, but yours seem to.

Gordon says no one could possibly resist proper porridge made by a real Scotsman.

Even I quite liked it, and I hate porridge.

I'd better go now. It's time for school.

I wish I could stay here and make cupcakes with Gordon.

But Mum says life isn't fair, even on the day before your birthday.

Love from

Eddie

PS Emily says can you send a picture of the lambs.

PPS Please say hello to Mr McDougall from me.

From: Edward Smith–Pickle

To: Morton Pickle

Date: Friday 24 March

Subject: Where are you????

 Attachments: Quiet night in; Popcorn problem

Dear Uncle Morton

Mum says thanks very much for ruining her one chance of happiness.

Gordon has gone for a walk. He said, "See you later," but Mum says he'll probably just drive straight back to Scotland.

I think they had a bit of a row.

It was Ziggy's fault. Or maybe Arthur's.

I don't know which of them bit the babysitter.

Mum found one who did pets. She booked another table at that French restaurant. She was wearing her second–favourite dress and Gordon was in his suit again.

Emily and I waved them goodbye on the doorstep.

Then we stayed here and watched telly with the babysitter.

Everything was going fine till she got hungry.

She should have known you never take popcorn from a dragon.

When the smoke cleared, the babysitter was jumping around on one leg, screaming at the top of her voice and looking for her phone.

Mum and Gordon had to come straight home. They didn't even get to try their starter.

Now Ziggy and Arthur are back on the patio.

They both look very sad.

They're staring through the glass, watching Mum eat their Maltesers.

She's going to put them on the train to Scotland if you're not here first thing tomorrow morning.

I don't like the idea of two dragons alone on the train, but Mum says they're old enough to look after themselves.

Please get here soon.

Eddie

From: Morton Pickle

To: Edward Smith-Pickle

Date: Friday 24 March

Subject: Re: Where are you????

Dear Eddie

You can tell your mother not to worry.
I have just booked a flight from Glasgow,
leaving at nine o'clock tomorrow morning.
I should be with you just after lunch.

I am very much looking forward to wishing
you happy birthday in person.

If your mother will allow me and the
dragons to stay for the afternoon, I shall
have a chance to see your magician in
action.

Unfortunately I appear to have mislaid your
invitation. Can you remind me what time
the party starts?

Finally – and most importantly – what would you like for your birthday? I'm ashamed to say that I have failed to buy you anything, but if you could give me a suggestion for the perfect gift, I shall try to find it at the airport.

Love from

your affectionate uncle

Morton

From: Edward Smith-Pickle

To: Morton Pickle

Date: Saturday 25 March

Subject: 3pm

Attachments: Opening my presents

Dear Uncle Morton

The party starts at 3 o'clock.

Please try to get here on time or you'll miss Mister Mysterio sawing someone in half.

I'm very pleased my friends will get to meet you.

Don't worry about not getting me a birthday present. Dad didn't either.

He didn't even send me a card. He just texted me this morning.

Mum said that was typical of him, which isn't actually true because last year he sent me a new bike.

I think he's just very busy at the moment rebuilding his castle.

If you would like to get me something, I would really like a magic set.

I did ask Mum for one, but she gave me a microscope and a book and another book and three pairs of socks instead.

Gordon gave me a fishing rod.

I always thought fishing was a bit boring, but he says nothing could be further from the truth.

He wanted to teach me this morning, but Mum said not when nineteen kids are arriving any minute.

They're not really arriving any minute. It's only ten past eight.

But we do have a lot of clearing up to do before the party starts, not to mention making the sandwiches, opening the bags of crisps and putting all the sausage rolls on plates.

So I'd better go.

See you later!

Love from

Eddie

From: Edward Smith-Pickle

To: Morton Pickle

Date: Saturday 25 March

Subject: My party

 **Attachments:** Party pics

Dear Uncle Morton

Did you miss your flight?

You missed a great party too.

I thought it was great, anyway, although I'm not sure everyone did.

Mister Mysterio certainly didn't.

The problem was he didn't listen to me.

The first bit of his act went really well. First he made a coin disappear. Then he found it behind Emily's ear.

I said I could do that too.

Then he made ten coins disappear and he pulled a ten pound note out of Emily's nose.

He said, "Can you do that?"

I said I couldn't.

Then he asked me to pick a card, any card.

It was the Queen of Hearts.

He let me put the card back in the pack and shuffle them.

Then he took the pack and threw them in the air and just caught one of them – and it was the Queen of Hearts!

Then he made
a real goldfish
appear in a glass
of water.

Then he drank it
and the goldfish
appeared in
another glass.

Then he took off
his hat and put
his hand inside
and pulled out
a white rabbit.

I knew what would happen next. I had to warn Mister Mysterio. I shouted at him, "Put the rabbit back in the hat!"

"That's my next trick," he said. "First Henrietta is going to make some lettuce disappear."

He reached into his pocket and pulled out a handful of lettuce.

"*Bon appetit*, Henrietta," he said and gave the lettuce to the rabbit.

I shouted, "Look out! Behind you!"

Mister Mysterio just smiled. He said, "This is a magic show, not a pantomime. Let Henrietta eat her lettuce in peace."

She can't have taken more than a nibble before Ziggy swallowed her.

One gulp and she was gone.

For a moment, everyone was too surprised to speak.

Then Mister Mysterio went red in the face and started shouting at the top of his voice.

Mum said a self-respecting children's entertainer ought to be ashamed of himself for using language like that.

Mister Mysterio just shouted even louder.

He wanted Mum to pay eight hundred pounds to replace Henrietta.

Apparently it takes years to train a rabbit.

Emily said if he was such a good magician, why couldn't he magic the rabbit back again?

I thought that was actually quite a good suggestion, but Mister Mysterio took no notice.

He said if Mum didn't write him a cheque for eight hundred pounds plus his usual fee and expenses right now this minute he was going to call the police.

I think he really would have if Gordon hadn't taken him aside and had a few words.

I don't know what Gordon said, but Mister Mysterio went very quiet. He packed his suitcase and left without even saying goodbye.

I said maybe he could come back next year to saw Emily in half, and Mum said next year we're going to the cinema instead.

After that we should have had tea, but tea was cancelled because the dragons had eaten it.

The kitchen door was supposed to be kept shut at all times, but Mister Mysterio must have left it open when he collected his coat.

The dragons didn't leave anything, not even a single sausage roll.

Arthur even ate the candles from the top of the cake.

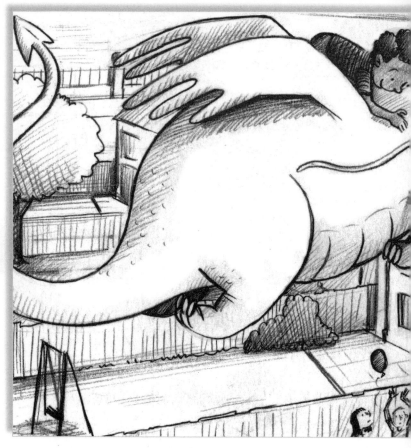

Luckily none of my friends minded, because we went into the garden and Ziggy let us take turns flying on her back.

Mum said please don't go too high or someone will fall off and she'll never be able to show her face in the playground again.

Ziggy took no notice. She flew my friend Sam to the roof of the house and left him there for twenty minutes while she was flying the rest of us around.

When Sam came down, he said it was the best birthday party ever.

I thought so too.

Love from

your one–year–older–than–yesterday
nephew

Eddie

From: Morton Pickle
To: Edward Smith–Pickle
Date: Saturday 25 March
Subject: Re: My party

Dear Eddie

You must imagine me clearing my throat and taking a deep breath, then bursting into song:

> *Happy birthday to you,*
> *Happy birthday to you,*
> *Happy birthday dear Eddie,*
> *Happy birthday to you!*

I am so sorry to have missed your party. We had a situation with one of the sheep last night, so it was impossible for me to catch my train to the airport this morning.

However, you will be glad to hear that her two lambs were delivered in perfect health just after nine o'clock this morning.

117

I have called them Eddie and Emily in your honour.

I have just looked at the trains and the flights. I could travel south tomorrow morning, but I would arrive at your house just as Gordon was leaving, which seems more than a little ridiculous. Would you mind looking after the dragons for one more night? Then he could bring them home in his car.

I have not forgotten your magic set, and I shall send it ASAP.

With much love and many happy returns

from your affectionate uncle

Morton

From: Edward Smith–Pickle

To: Morton Pickle

Date: Sunday 26 March

Subject: Magicians

Attachments: Hot bum

Dear Uncle Morton

I hope you haven't bought me a magic set for my birthday, because I don't want one after all.

I've decided I don't like magicians.

Today there was a knock at the door. It was Mister Mysterio.

He said he'd come for his money.

He kept shouting and waving his arms in the air.

Gordon said, "Why don't we calm down and talk about this like sensible people?"

Mister Mysterio said he'd had enough of talking. He just wanted his money.

Mum said he had to leave right now or she was going to call the police.

Mister Mysterio said he'd already done that himself, but they weren't interested. They told him that if he rang them with any more stories of rabbits and dragons, they would arrest him for wasting police time.

He said we'd have to sort this out between ourselves.

He said he wasn't going anywhere till we paid him.

He said he'd stay here all week if he had to.

He probably would have if Ziggy hadn't come to see what all the fuss was about.

That was when I realised Mister Mysterio wasn't a real magician.

A real magician would know it's not a good idea to shove a dragon.

For a moment, Ziggy stayed absolutely still.

All that moved was the smoke trickling out of her nostrils.

Then she went wild.

Mister Mysterio ran down the street with his bum on fire.

Gordon says he won't be coming back in a hurry.

Mum is worried he will, so she's asked Gordon to stay one more night.

She says can you carry on lambing?

Love from

Eddie

From: Morton Pickle
To: Edward Smith-Pickle
Date: Sunday 26 March
Subject: Re: Magicians

Dear Eddie

Please tell your mother that I am actually tremendously busy at the moment and can hardly spare any time away from my desk.

I should be preparing for my next trip abroad. I shall be travelling to Tibet to search for the yeti.

If Gordon is unable to return to Scotland tonight, I shall of course put my work aside and return to the lambs.

But I should be grateful if he could hurry home as soon as possible.

Morton

Dear Uncle Morton

You'll be glad to hear Gordon is loading his car now and his ETD is 8.15.

Mum is making him a Thermos of extra-strong coffee and some sandwiches.

I've made going-home bags for Ziggy and Arthur.

They've got chocolate buttons, gummy bears, cola bottles and lemon fizzes.

Gordon is going to drive all day. If the traffic isn't too bad, he and the dragons should be home in time for tea.

Love from

Eddie

PS If you don't know what ETD means, it means Estimated Time of Departure.

PPS Emily says please don't forget the photo of the lambs.

PPPS Your trip to Tibet sounds very interesting. Can I come too? I've always wanted to see a yeti.

PPPPS Have you ever read an email with so many PSs?

Dear Eddie

I'm very pleased to report that the dragons are safely back at home. As I write, Ziggy and Arthur are lying on the carpet at my feet, looking as happy as happy can be.

Junk food obviously suits them. I have rarely seen either of them looking so healthy. I shall have to ask Mrs McPherson in the Post Office to start stocking gummy bears.

Mr McDougall was delighted to see Gordon and sent him straight out to work in the fields. I believe he has delivered three lambs already.

I attach a picture for Emily.

You can tell her that these two lambs were helped into the world by her uncle and are now gambolling happily around Mr McDougall's fields.

For you, my dear nephew, I have put a small birthday present in the post. I'm sorry that it will be a couple of days late, but I hope you'll enjoy it anyway.

Thanks again for looking after the dragons so well.

With love from

your affectionate uncle

Morton

From: Edward Smith–Pickle
To: Morton Pickle
Date: Wednesday 29 March
Subject: Your parcel

Attachments: My best present

Dear Uncle Morton

Thank you for the egg!

It's my best birthday present.

In fact, I think it's my best present ever.

I know you said it probably won't hatch, but I'm going to leave it in my sock drawer anyway.

Then if a dragon does come out, it will be nice and cosy.

Please say hello to Ziggy and Arthur from me. I hope you're keeping them away from the lambs.

Emily says thank you for the picture and she has never seen anything so cute.

Mum is a bit sad. I think she's missing Gordon. If you see him, please ask him to come and see us again soon.

The dragons are invited too, of course.

Love from

Eddie

Barnacle, Mullet & Crabbe Solicitors

147 Lordship Lane, London EC1V 2AX
bcrabbe@barnaclemulletcrabbe.com

Thursday 30 March

Dear Mr Pickle

I have been instructed by my client, Barry Daniels, also known as The Amazing Mister Mysterio, to pursue a claim for damages against you and your pet or pets.

Our client was booked to perform a magic show at the birthday party of Edward Smith-Pickle on Saturday 25 March.

He had performed a little less than half of his usual routine when a creature, species unknown, pushed him aside and ate his rabbit, Henrietta.

Our client has been informed that the creature belongs to you and therefore you bear full responsibility for its actions and their consequences.

Our client will accept a minimum payment of eight hundred pounds for the loss of his rabbit.

Henrietta had undergone two years of intensive training and had assisted our client in more than seventy magic shows. His business has been severely disrupted by her loss.

Our client also wishes to be reimbursed for his full fee and expenses for the magic show.

Finally our client wishes to be reimbursed for one pair of brown trousers which were damaged in a fire caused by your pet or pets.

A bill is enclosed.

Our client would be grateful for payment of the full sum within seven days.

Yours sincerely

Bartholomew Crabbe

Senior Partner
Barnacle, Mullet and Crabbe

From: Morton Pickle

To: Bartholomew Crabbe

Date: Friday 31 March

Subject: Henrietta

 Attachments: Bunnies

Dear Mr Crabbe

Thank you for your letter about your client, Barry Daniels, also known as The Amazing Mister Mysterio.

I was very sorry to hear about Henrietta and her unfortunate accident. As an animal-lover myself, I can appreciate how upsetting it must have been for your client.

I shall, of course, provide him with a replacement, although I would rather not pay eight hundred pounds. That does seem awfully expensive for a rabbit, however well-trained.

I have an abundance of rabbits on my island. They are always eating my lettuces. Mister Mysterio is welcome to take as many as he wants.

Perhaps he could teach me some magic at the same time.

I have spoken to my sister, who told me that she has already sent a cheque to Mr Daniels for his fee and expenses.

I suggested that she should only pay half his fee, since he only performed half his magic, but she has paid the full amount.

If I were Mr Daniels, I should think myself very lucky.

With all best wishes

Morton Pickle

Party Cupcakes

Gordon doesn't just make tasty porridge – he's also a star baker! Ask an adult to help you make these delicious cupcakes next time you're having a party.

You will need:

- 110 grams butter, softened
- 110 grams caster sugar
- 2 eggs, beaten (chicken, not dragon)
- 1 teaspoon vanilla extract
- 110 grams self–raising flour, sifted
- 1–2 tablespoons of milk
- Writing icing pens
- Silver balls
- Scales
- Cupcake tin with 12 holes
- Cupcake paper cases
- Bowl
- Hand mixer
- Metal spoon
- Oven
- Oven gloves
- Skewer

1 Set the oven to 180°C/350F and line the tin with paper cases.

2 Beat the butter and sugar together in a bowl with the hand mixer until pale and creamy.

3 Dribble in the beaten egg slowly as you mix. Then add the vanilla extract.

4 Use a metal spoon to fold in the flour.

5 Add a little milk to make the mixture a bit more runny. It should drop off a spoon.

6 Divide the mixture between the cases, making sure they are only half-full.

7 Get an adult to help you put the tin in the oven. Bake for 10–15 minutes, until the cakes are light brown and risen to the top of the cases.

8 Wearing oven gloves, take the cakes out of the oven and test one with a skewer – if it comes out clean, the cake is done. Remove the cakes from the tin and leave to cool on a rack for a couple of hours.

9 Now you can have fun decorating your cupcakes! Why not use a green writing icing pen to draw a fierce dragon head, and use silver balls for eyes?

Dragonsitter Wordsearch

Answer the questions below then find the words in the wordsearch opposite.

(**Hint:** the number of spaces shows how many letters there are in each answer.)

1. What colour is Ziggy the dragon?

_ _ _ _ _

2. What is the name of Eddie's uncle?

_ _ _ _ _ _

3. What is a dragon's favourite food?

_ _ _ _ _ _ _ _ _

4. What is Eddie's surname?

_ _ _ _ _ — _ _ _ _ _

5. What is the name of Mr McDougall's nephew?

_ _ _ _ _ _

136

6. Where does Eddie's uncle live?

_ _ _ _ _ _ _

7. How do Eddie and his uncle talk to each other?

_ _ _ _ _

8. What is Ziggy's baby called?

_ _ _ _ _ _

C	P	M	K	C	R	A	X	X	L	C	T
C	H	S	W	A	R	T	H	U	R	C	F
D	A	O	Q	Y	L	U	W	J	D	B	J
X	T	A	C	X	G	O	R	D	O	N	Z
M	O	R	T	O	N	M	N	P	G	G	P
I	V	H	A	O	L	A	J	G	E	W	Q
W	D	A	K	K	L	A	Y	R	K	D	D
K	R	V	W	T	G	T	T	E	P	X	E
Q	K	B	O	R	M	F	S	E	W	H	S
I	V	C	F	T	E	S	H	N	N	T	A
B	S	M	I	T	H	P	I	C	K	L	E
L	U	V	E	M	A	I	L	W	S	X	L

Could You Be a Dragonsitter?

Have you got what it takes to be a brilliant dragonsitter? Answer these questions to find out!

1 You've just got your dragon. But she's hungry! What will you feed her?

a Frozen chips. She can cook her own food, surely?

b Your little sister. That solves that problem.

c Chocolate! It's what you'd have for tea if you could.

2 Your dragon needs the loo, but she can't fit on it! Where's the next best place to take her?

a Behind the sofa. No one will notice for a while.

b In your mum's bedroom. What can go wrong?

c In the back garden, though mind the goldfish pond.

3 Your dragon is getting restless. Time for some exercise. But what kind?

a Take her to the park playground. She can almost fit on the slide.

b Let her chase your big brother – he needs a run around anyway.

c Put her outside for a quick fly around the garden after tea.

4 Now it's bedtime. Where is your dragon going to sleep?

a On the kitchen floor, there's plenty of room there.

b In the freezer, she must get hot in the night.

c In your bed, though it might be a bit of a squeeze.

5 There's a bit of a surprise the next day — she's laid an egg! But what should you do with an extremely rare dragon's egg?

a Post it to the local museum, they might want it.

b Well, it's breakfast time, so omelette for everyone!

c Wrap it up carefully in your sock drawer to keep it warm.

Spot the
Difference

Here are two pictures. There are six differences on the second picture – can you circle them all?

Dragonsitter Jokes

Roar with laughter at these beastly jokes!

What happened when Eddie took Ziggy to the pet show?

She was beast in show

What sound do you hear when the dragons eat curry?

The fire alarm

What's a dragon's favourite snack?

Firecrackers

What do you get when a dragon sneezes?

Out of the way

What's a hungry dragon's favourite day of the week?

Chewsday

Why do dragons sleep during the day?

So they can fight knights

What did the adult dragon say to the baby dragon?

'You're too young to smoke!'

What's big and scaly and bounces?

A dragon on a trampoline

What do you get if you cross a yeti with Dracula?

Frostbite

What did the Loch Ness Monster say to her friend?

'Long time no sea!'

What do you call an underwater dinosaur wearing a skirt?

The Loch Dress Monster

What do you get if you cross an elephant with the abominable snowman?

A jumbo yeti

What do you get if you cross the Loch Ness Monster with a shark?

Loch Jaws

How do you talk to the Loch Ness Monster?

Drop her a line

Why are dragons good storytellers?

They have some tails to tell

143

Your holiday homework:

Choose a country and write 10 interesting facts about it.

Your name: _Edward Smith-Pickle_

Your teacher: _Miss Brackenbury_

The country that you have chosen:
Mongolia

Your 10 facts:

1 Mongolia is a large country which you will find between Russia and China.

2 Ulaanbaatar is the capital of Mongolia and the largest city in the country.

3 Ulaanbaatar has a population of over one million people.

4 Mongolia is bigger than Germany, France, and the UK added together, but only three million people live there. If you added together the populations of Germany, France and the UK, you would have more than two hundred million people.

5 Most people in Mongolia are Buddhist.

6 The national drink is called airag.
It is made from horse's milk.

7 The Gobi Desert is in Mongolia.

8 Many people in Mongolia live in big round tents called yurts.

9 Some of the animals that live in Mongolia are: snow leopards, camels, yaks, dragons.

10 The dragons in Mongolia live mostly in caves in the highest mountains in the country.

Thank you for this lovely work, Eddie. You have found some very interesting facts about Mongolia. You have used good vocabulary and excellent imagination.

Suggestions for improvements: have a look at our notes from last term on the difference between fiction and non-fiction.

Miss Brackenbury

From: Morton Pickle

To: Alice Brackenbury

Date: Tuesday 28 March

Subject: Book launch

Attachments: Invitation

Dear Miss Brackenbury

My publishers are throwing a small party to celebrate the publication of my new book, and I wondered if you might like to join us.

My nephew Eddie will be there along with his sister and mother. I'm sure you see enough of Eddie at school, but there should be some other entertaining people at the party, including our guest of honour, the renowned Professor Baast, one of Mongolia's foremost naturalists.

I'm terribly sorry that I haven't had a chance to talk to your students about my adventures yet, but I'm exceedingly busy at the moment. My next book will be about my hunt for the yeti in Tibet.

146

I have been there on several previous occasions without catching so much as a glimpse of the elusive beast; I'm hoping for better luck this time around. If I do manage to see it, perhaps I could come and describe it to your students?

Please do let me know if you are able to come to the party. It would be a great pleasure to meet you there.

With all best wishes,

Morton

The directors of Flugge Press
invite you to celebrate the publication of

The Winged Serpents
✦ of Zavkhan ✦

In Search of the Dragons of Outer Mongolia
by Morton Pickle

at The Explorers Club, Pall Mall, London
on Wednesday 10 May from 6.30 to 8.30pm
RSVP eve@fluggepress.com

The Winged Serpents of Zavkhan

 ## INTRODUCTION

I shall never forget the first moment that I set eyes on a dragon, not least because I believed that its own dark cold eyes were the last thing I was ever going to see.

I had been trekking through the most inhospitable mountains of Mongolia for more than a week with my dear friend, the well-known naturalist, Douglas Macalister.

A terrible storm had raged for the previous three days. Visibility was almost zero. Our guide had deserted us, returning to his village, claiming that flying beasts inhabited this region, snatching untended sheep and even small children. We did not believe him, of course, considering his fears to be no more than uneducated superstition.

Despite our entreaties, the guide had taken his animals, leaving us with nothing but a weary old donkey who could barely drag herself up the mountainside, let alone the bags strapped to her flanks. Our supplies had run low.

We sustained ourselves with mouthfuls of snow. The nearest village couldn't have been less than two days' walk away. As far as we knew, there was not a living creature for miles around. Doom beckoned.

By dusk on the third day of the storm, all seemed lost, and probably would have been, had Douglas not spotted a darkness in the mountainside. To our astonishment and delight, we realised that this slim shadow was the entrance to a cave. We slipped inside and stood in the silence, out of the bitter wind and the endless driving snow, thanking our good fortune.

We had been standing there for only a few moments, both of us grinning wildly with relief and exhaustion, when a strange shuffling came from the back of the cave, and a dazzling flash of flame suddenly illuminated the gloom.

To read more about Morton Pickle's extraordinary adventures, please purchase a copy of his new book The Winged Serpents of Zavkhan: In Search of the Dragons of Outer Mongolia. *Available in all good book shops.*

Answers

P136

1. Green
2. Morton
3. Chocolate
4. Smith-Pickle
5. Gordon
6. Scotland
7. Email
8. Arthur

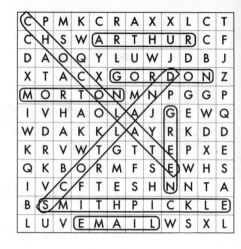

P138

If you got...

Mostly As – Nearly there! You've got the right general idea, but some of your answers might need further thought – if you leave your dragon in the kitchen, she will eat all your food, and she'll probably scare the other kids in the park if you take her out!

Mostly Bs – Oh dear, you need to go back to dragonsitting school! All of your answers will go horribly wrong – Mum is not going to like finding dragon dung in her room, and there's no way she'll let you feed your sister to your new pet! Try again!

Mostly Cs – Good job, dragonsitter! Your answers should give you a happy, healthy dragon, and hopefully you won't annoy anyone else, even if you need a lie-in the next day!

P140

The Dragonsitter

Josh Lacey

Illustrated by Garry Parsons

'Dear Uncle Morton, you'd better get on a plane right now and come back here. Your dragon has eaten Jemima. Emily loved that rabbit.'

It had sounded so easy: Eddie was going to look after Uncle Morton's unusual pet for a week while he went on holiday. But soon the fridge is empty, the curtains are blazing, and the postman is fleeing down the garden path.

'This witty book deserves to be read and reread'
Books for Keeps

9781849394192 £4.99

The Dragonsitter Takes Off

Josh Lacey

Illustrated by Garry Parsons

'Dear Uncle Morton, Ziggy won't move from the linen cupboard. He still hasn't eaten a thing. Not even a Malteser. I'm really quite worried about him.'

Eddie had thought that this time dragonsitting would be easy – until Ziggy disappears, only to be found in the linen cupboard, refusing to budge. But moving Ziggy is the last thing on Eddie's mind when he learns that his uncle's dragon has been keeping a big secret . . .

'A brilliant follow up for all of Eddie and Ziggy's fans'
Julia Eccleshare, Lovereading

9781849395717 £4.99

The Dragonsitter's Castle

Josh Lacey
Illustrated by Garry Parsons

'Dear Uncle Morton, your dragons are still here. They have eaten the entire contents of the fridge and most of the tins in the cupboard too.

Arthur also swallowed three spoons and the remote control. Mum says they will probably come out the other end, but I'm not really looking forward to that.'

Dragonsitting isn't getting any easier for Eddie. A castle, a sneezing dragon and a big box of fireworks. Looks like the new year is going to start with a bang!

Praise for *The Dragonsitter*:
'Short, sharp and funny'
Telegraph

9781849397698 £4.99